UNDER FIRE

GABRIELLE PRENDERGAST

UNDER FIRE

ORCA BOOK PUBLISHERS

Copyright © Gabrielle Prendergast 2025

Published in Canada and the United States
in 2025 by Orca Book Publishers.
orcabook.com

All rights are reserved, including those for text and data mining, AI training and similar technologies. No part of this publication may be reproduced or transmitted in any form or by any means, electronic or mechanical, including photocopying, recording or by any information storage and retrieval system now known or to be invented, without permission in writing from the publisher. The publisher expressly prohibits the use of this work in connection with the development of any software program, including, without limitation, training a machine-learning or generative artificial intelligence (AI) system.

Library and Archives Canada Cataloguing in Publication
Title: Under fire / Gabrielle Prendergast.
Names: Prendergast, Gabrielle, author.
Series: Orca anchor.
Description: Series statement: Orca anchor
Identifiers: Canadiana (print) 20240412141 | Canadiana (ebook) 2024041215x |
ISBN 9781459838222 (softcover) | ISBN 9781459840294 (PDF) |
ISBN 9781459840300 (EPUB)
Subjects: LCGFT: Novels.
Classification: LCC PS8631.R448 U53 2025 | DDC jC813/.6—dc23

Library of Congress Control Number: 2024939990

Summary: In this high-interest accessible novel for teen readers, sixteen-year-old Poppy and her brother are home alone when a nearby wildfire builds and threatens to burn down their farm.

Orca Book Publishers is committed to reducing the consumption of nonrenewable resources in the production of our books. We make every effort to use materials that support a sustainable future.

Orca Book Publishers gratefully acknowledges the support for its publishing programs provided by the following agencies: the Government of Canada, the Canada Council for the Arts and the Province of British Columbia through the BC Arts Council and the Book Publishing Tax Credit.

Design by Ella Collier.
Edited by Sara Cassidy.
Cover photography by Getty Images/Nika Fadul and Unsplash/Egor Vikhrev.
Author photo by Erika Forest.

Printed and bound in Canada.

28 27 26 25 • 1 2 3 4

Chapter One

Living on a farm was supposed to mean fresh air and sunshine. That was the idea anyway.

When Mom died, we got some money from her life insurance. And then Dad sold our apartment. It seemed like a lot of money. But Dad said it wasn't enough to buy anything decent in Vancouver.

His idea was that we would start again. Without Mom. Without being in the place where she'd been so sick. For so long.

It's not like we were going to forget her. But we didn't need to be reminded every minute. Every time we looked at the spot where her oxygen tank had sat. Or the scratch on the wall made by her wheelchair. The cupboard where she'd kept all her pills.

It was cancer. And it was bad. Medical supplies and machines and nurses. And poor Mom, trying to smile through it all.

Farm life was supposed to be the opposite of all that.

Mom died nearly three years ago. And now we've been on the farm for one year.

We're having carrot cake today to celebrate. But no fresh air. And no sunshine.

Just wildfire smoke.

"I don't think it's even cloudy today," my brother, Jed, says. He squints up at the hazy, gray sky.

"Close the door," Dad says. He digs around in a drawer. "Poppy, do we have a cake server?"

"Yes, close it, Jed," I say. "You're letting the smoky air in. The cake server is in the second drawer," I tell Dad.

"So many wildfires this year," Jed says. "It's because of climate change." He's been saying that every day for the past month. He closes the door.

Dad serves the cake. We use mismatched plates. And teacups from a thrift store. Mom didn't like new things. We brought all her kitchen stuff with us.

Some reminders are okay.

I wish I still fit the clothes she bought me. But I was only thirteen when she died. Not even full-grown.

I still like to shop at the thrift stores in Vernon or Kamloops. But it's hard without her. I don't know what to choose. Or what looks good on me.

Dad's no help. He says I look pretty in everything. And I can't ask Jed. He just laughs.

"Poppy, can I have more cake?" Jed asks.

"You haven't finished what you have," I say.

Jed looks at the half-eaten cake slice on his plate. "Oh," he says.

Jed is two years older than me. But he needs help sometimes.

He has a disability. His body is fine. Strong even. He's good at working on the farm. With the animals. And in the garden.

It's an intellectual disability. It's not autism. It's not Down syndrome. His brain is just different. Some things are hard for him. He needed a lot of support in school. He struggles to read. He can't do even simple math.

Dad says Jed will never live on his own. But that's why we moved to the farm.

Jed loves animals. And being outdoors. So Dad made a plan for Jed's future.

He bought the farm. Now Jed's done with school, he'll work on it. Soon we'll have support workers to help. Dad will do his sales job online. And I just finished tenth grade at the little school in Enderby. It suits me. My school in Vancouver wasn't very good.

"To a successful year!" Dad says. He raises his teacup. Jed and I raise ours. We clink them together.

It *has* been a successful year. When we got to the farm, there was nothing here. Just an old house. The barn was falling down. No livestock. No garden.

But now we have a dozen chickens. A very sweet mare named Biscuit. A less sweet donkey called Itchy. This spring we got eight sheep—all ewes. And a sheepdog named Candi to watch over them.

The garden that Jed planted is looking lush. We've picked tomatoes, beans, carrots. We'll be able to harvest more soon.

Most important, Dad had enough money to build a new steel barn. It's solar-powered and ultramodern. And it's heated so the animals will be warm in the winter. It's even air-conditioned if it gets too hot in the summer. The animals have a nicer house than we do!

It was strange to leave my friends. My school. Some of Mom's friends didn't think we should leave the city. They thought it was reckless. But Dad believed it would save our family.

Dad and Jed clear the table. I wash up while Dad watches Jed brush his teeth. Through the window above the sink, I can see wildfire smoke. It looks like clouds. But I know it's not.

Dad says the fires are far away. We're not in danger here. I still worry though.

Since Mom died, nothing feels certain or safe. Not the farm. Not Dad. Not Jed.

And not me.

Chapter Two

Farm days begin at dawn. But it's still dark when Dad's phone rings. It wakes me. I hear him stumbling around. He talks in a low voice.

By the time I get out of bed, Jed is up too.

"What's going on?" I ask. Dad is drinking milk straight from the carton. I nearly say, "Get a glass!" That's what Mom would say. I press my lips together.

"The fire spread overnight," Dad says. "They need me in Salmon Arm. To help with a back burn."

"What's a back burn?" Jed asks.

Dad tosses the empty milk carton into the recycling bin.

"A back burn is a controlled fire. We burn a section of brush on purpose. That helps control the direction of a wildfire. To keep it away from the town."

"Have you done that before?" I ask. "It sounds dangerous."

"I did it when I was in the army," Dad says. "It's less dangerous than fighting the fire directly."

I help Dad find his boots and work gloves. Jed disappears back into his room. But when

Dad heads out the door, Jed comes out. He's dressed in work clothes. He's carrying a full pack.

"I'll come," he says.

Dad and I look at each other. It's hard to disappoint Jed.

"I'm afraid you can't come, Jed," Dad says. "I'm picking up Mr. Chin and his farmhands up the road. There won't be room in the car. Besides, you need to look after Poppy."

"I don't need—" I start to object. But then I realize Dad is trying to spare Jed's feelings. "I mean, exactly. I don't want to be here alone."

Jed rolls his eyes. He's not fooled.

"I need help with the animals," I add. "I can't manage them all by myself."

"Well, that's true," Jed says. He's very possessive of the animals. He says he named all the sheep and chickens. But he won't tell me their names.

"There," Dad says. He hoists his pack. Jed goes back to his room. I walk Dad out to the car.

"Keep your phone charged," he says. "I'll call every couple of hours. And…" He looks up to the house. "Take care of your brother. He knows his chores. But make sure he eats. And don't let him tire out Biscuit or Candi. I've left the keys for the truck on the hook. Don't let Jed drive it."

Back in the kitchen, Jed has laid out three cereal bowls. As he opens a fresh carton of milk, I quietly put one bowl away. Sometimes

I'm not sure if he just can't count or if he forgets that Mom is gone.

When we're done eating, he heads back outside. "I'm going to mow a firebreak," he says. "In the hay field and around the house."

Jed is allowed to drive the ride-on mower. It's electric and has no gears. One of his chores is mowing the large lawn at the front of the house. He does a great job.

It's hard to predict what Jed will be good at. Or what he will struggle with. It's always been like that.

"How do you know about firebreaks?" I ask.

"YouTube," he says, disappearing out the door. I resist the urge to follow him. To supervise. I know this is something Jed can manage. I have to let him have some independence.

I decide to check on the animals. I smell the smoke as I step outside.

The chickens are in their yard. They happily dig for worms and bugs. We have organic chicken feed for them. But they seem to prefer wild food. They cluck and scuttle around my feet. I check that their water dispenser is full.

In their coop, I gather the eggs. One each from all twelve chickens. We get that almost every day. We sell most of them to a market store up the road. Dad is so pleased. He plans to get another ten or twelve chickens in the spring. We can always use more income. Every little bit counts.

I stop at the gate to the big pasture. Biscuit, our horse, comes over. She nudges me with her nose.

Biscuit loves people. Jed especially. He took horse-riding lessons when he was young. So he's very good with her.

I took a few lessons too. Not as many as Jed. His were free because of an adaptive riding charity. They pay for kids like Jed to have riding lessons. Mom and Dad had to pay for mine. It was expensive. I only did a couple of years.

I've had more practice since we've been on the farm. I'm not as good as Jed, but Biscuit likes me.

She is not a fan of the sheep.

They're in the other pasture with Itchy, the donkey. Itchy is bad-tempered but good at keeping the sheep safe. Once Dad heard a commotion in the sheep paddock at night. When he rushed out there, all he saw was a fox limping away. And Itchy huffing angrily.

I'm not sure Itchy even likes the sheep. I think he protects them more as a matter of pride. His only friend is Candi, the sheepdog. She sometimes sleeps on his back.

Candi bounds up to the fence to greet me. That startles the sheep. They baa at her and run off in all directions.

"Oh be quiet," I tell them. Candi barks and chases after them. She gathers them back into a tight group. As a sheepdog, that's her instinct. She can't resist doing it.

The sheep gaze up at me when they settle down.

"You'll be meeting Mr. Chin's ram soon," I say to them. "And then, in the spring, you'll all have babies. Won't that be exciting?"

They don't look very excited. Not as excited as I am anyway. We're going to sell the lambs. If each of our sheep has one or two, we'll earn enough to pay for my first semester of college. That's what Dad told me.

Like I said, every little bit counts.

Chapter Three

I help Jed weed the garden. By lunchtime our throats are dry and irritated from the smoke.

"It's getting worse," Jed says. He stands next to the potato patch, hands on his hips, face turned to the sky. In his overalls and rubber boots, he looks every bit a farmer.

I wasn't sure about Dad's plan for the farm. He seemed to think it was the right choice for Jed. And Dad grew up on a farm. He knew Jed would be happy here.

No one really asked me.

But seeing Jed so at home reassures me. He had a lot of trouble at school in Vancouver. Classes were hard for him. And he got bullied. It was such a big school, no one seemed to notice.

Then he got hidden away in the special ed class.

The school in Enderby was a lot better for him. It's small. Everyone knows everyone. Jed got more help.

It's good for me too. There's less fighting.

Less troublemaking. I can concentrate on my work.

I have two more years of school. And by then we'll have saved enough for me to go away to college. That's my dream.

I want to study to be an EAL teacher. Then I can work in China or Poland or Brazil. I've always wanted to travel.

I used to read books about different countries. The idea was exciting. But also kind of scary. After losing Mom, I'm not feeling very brave.

I don't want to give up on my dream, though. Traveling from Vancouver to the farm was like a baby step. And I survived. So far, so good.

If it weren't for the smoky air, I'd be feeling pretty optimistic about things.

We eat lunch in the house. When we're done eating, I remind Jed to brush his teeth again. Then he does one of his speech exercises with the computer. I listen to him as I tidy the kitchen and do some other chores.

"May-mee-my-moe-moo." He repeats it really loud, then quiet, then medium, then quiet again. Jed has trouble controlling the volume of his voice. These exercises are supposed to help. I don't know whether they work. But doing the exercises seems to relax him.

Anyway, out on the farm, who cares how loud he talks?

When he's done, we take a break and watch *Maui Rescue* together. The house feels uncomfortably warm. We both fan ourselves with bits of cardboard.

As an episode of *Maui Rescue* ends, Jed opens the back door. Smoke wafts in. "Oh no," I say, leaping up.

Outside, we can barely see the hills above the paddocks.

"The animals!" Jed cries. He runs into the smoke before I can stop him. I follow. The kitchen door slams closed behind me.

When we get to the paddocks, the animals are agitated. Candi barks. She has herded the sheep into the corner of the field by the gate. Itchy hee-haws angrily. The chickens seem listless. They might think it's nighttime. The sky is dark from the smoke.

"Will the smoke hurt the animals?" Jed asks.

"I don't know," I say. The air smells heavy and sour. My nose and eyes sting. "Let's get them all into the barn. We can turn on the air-conditioning. It has filters."

"Good idea," Jed says.

I run to the veggie garden. I grab a handful of beet leaves. I scatter them along the path to the barn. The chickens love beet leaves. They follow the path happily, gobbling the beet leaves as they go.

Jed whistles three times. Candi understands what this means. She jumps into action. She herds the sheep out of their paddock. They trot down the path. Minutes later they're in the barn too. Jed throws a bale down from the hayloft for them to eat.

Itchy finds his own way to the barn. He immediately starts chasing the sheep. Jed sprinkles some oats around to distract him.

I go back for Biscuit. But she proves to be a challenge.

"Biscuit!" I yell out into the paddock. She neighs back. But she stays away from the gate.

The smoke and fuss have made her skittish. I chase her around the paddock until I'm out of breath and my throat is raw. I bend over and cough. Jed brings me a bottle of water.

"I'll ride her in," he says.

"She's not saddled."

"She's wearing a bridle," Jed points out. "I can ride bareback."

"That's dangerous, isn't it?"

Jed rolls his eyes. "I'm not going to gallop. Or even trot. We'll walk in."

Biscuit comes straight to Jed. He talks gently to her. I watch from the gate. Then he grabs the bridle straps and hoists himself up. Seconds later he's calmly riding her through the gate. I follow them into the barn.

Biscuit settles with the rest of the animals. I grab some soft drinks from the house. I stop to make some sandwiches too. On the way out the door, I pause. Grabbing a bag, I pack the sandwiches and two water bottles. I add some fruit and other snacks. I'm not sure why. It just seems smart.

The smoke stings my eyes on the way back.

With the air filters on, it's much easier to

breathe in the barn. We eat some snacks. We watch Candi play with Itchy, chasing him around. Jed gives Biscuit a good brush. I watch him, thinking.

It's not that I mind farmwork. It took a while to learn. Now I've gotten used to it. But when I see Jed with the animals, he looks so at ease. So happy. I feel a little left out. Like I don't fit.

Mom used to worry about Jed because of his disability. She wondered if he would ever have a job. When she got cancer, we started to worry about her instead.

I wish Mom could see Jed now. With the animals. Or in his garden.

Sometimes I think that the farm is Mom's gift to Jed. And to Dad. And me too, I guess.

I imagine her looking down from heaven and saying, *This is for all of you.*

"Is the smoke bothering your eyes, Poppy?" Jed asks. Biscuit flicks her nose at me.

I wipe my tears away quickly. "No, I'm fine," I say.

Chapter Four

Dad has sent five texts so far.

8 am: Arrived at fire. It looks worse than it is.

10:30 am: We're moving to south of town. There's another fire in the cliffs.

2 pm: The hill fire is bad. If you hear planes it's the water bombers. Don't worry.

4:15 pm: I'm helping evacuate south of town. People calm but worried.

5:10 pm: We're taking a dinner break. Traffic jam heading south.

Jed picks some ripe cherry tomatoes from his garden. We eat them with our sandwiches in the barn.

"It doesn't look good out there," he says when he comes back. I take my sandwich to one of the windows and look out. The stream of smoke in the hills looks closer.

Turning back, I look at Jed and the animals milling around the barn. What if the fire comes here?

The barn is steel, so it might not burn. But if we're inside, we'll be cooked. Literally.

I toss the rest of my sandwich to Itchy. He eats it in two bites.

"I'm going to get the truck," I say.

Jed looks up from his dinner. "What for?"

"Just in case. We might need to leave in a hurry," I say. I walk out before he can argue.

I grab Candi's dog crate from the house. It's heavy. But I manage to lift it into the back of the truck. Most of the chickens will fit in there. We also have two travel carriers, a large one that we use for Candi and a smaller one that two or three chickens can fit in. I grab them.

Jed and I can evacuate in the truck. And we can take Candi and the chickens.

I open the large barn doors and drive the truck in through them.

Jed sees the crate and the carriers in the back of the truck.

"Just in case?" he says.

"Yes."

He nods grimly. "I'm going to turn the lawn and garden sprinklers on."

"Be careful." I almost cry as he leaves. Turning the sprinklers on is a sensible idea. Our sprinkler system is fed by a stream. Even though the water level is low, it will keep running. It could save the house. And the garden.

The chickens get into the crate and carriers peacefully. I think they're tired and want to go to sleep. I load them all into the back of the truck and cover them with a tarp.

Biscuit, Itchy and the sheep seem to be watching me. I can't look at them. Am I going to leave them behind? To burn?

Seconds after Jed gets back, my phone rings. It's Dad.

"The fire missed Salmon Arm," he says. "But the one in the hills is a problem. It could head your way."

"I saw the smoke," I tell him. "It is getting thicker. And closer."

Jed crouches and puts his arms around Candi. Candi whines.

"It's moving fast," Dad says. "I want you and Jed to take the truck. Go along the valley road. Take the river turnoff. Cross the bridge. Then drive south toward Lumby. I don't think the fire will jump the river."

My heart is pounding. Even though I was planning for this, it doesn't seem real.

"I can't get back," Dad says. "The highway is jammed. People are trying to turn around now that Salmon Arm is safe."

"Where should we go?" I ask.

"The truck's gas tank is full," Dad says. "You remember how to get to Granny's place in Vernon on the back road, right? Go there."

The "scenic route," Dad usually calls it. Along a prettier road than the highway, Vernon is at least an hour away. And that's driving in a car or truck. Not leading a flock of sheep, a donkey and a horse.

"What about the animals?" I ask.

Dad is silent for a moment. "Take Candi. Put the chickens in the truck. Then leave the barn and all the gates open. Itchy and Biscuit are smart. They'll run away from the fire. Hopefully the sheep will follow them."

"But what if they don't?"

"We have insurance, Poppy," Dad says. He doesn't add, *They're only animals*. I know he's thinking it. After all, we were planning on selling their lambs as food.

But that feels wrong to me. The sheep are part of the farm. They are part of our family.

I don't tell Dad I have a different plan.

Chapter Five

"The valley road is super slow to drive down anyway," I tell Jed.

It's a gravel road. Bumpy and rutted and dusty. "We'll barely be slower with all the animals. I'll drive the chickens in the truck. Can you ride Biscuit?"

"Of course," Jed says. "But—"

I interrupt him. "Put Itchy on a lead to follow you. The sheep will follow Itchy. Candi will keep them together. Once we get across the river, we will find somewhere to leave them."

Jed does not like my plan. Then he changes his mind and thinks it's the best plan ever. Back and forth. Three times in the last ten minutes. He's like that sometimes. Especially when he's anxious.

I fight to put a harness on Itchy. Jed saddles Biscuit. I pack water and as much food as I can. For us and the animals. Jed helps. He checks the truck's emergency kit. He brings extra water bottles. A flashlight. A blanket.

Emergency planning is another one of Jed's interests. Animals, gardening and emergencies.

It's evening when we set out. The sun will set in two hours. But it's already dark from the smoke. The air smells awful.

I steer the truck out through the barn door. Candi barks. The sheep obediently trail after us into the yard. Jed leads Biscuit and Itchy out of the barn. He closes up the big doors.

I drive slowly past our house to the road. I can't help but wonder if this is the last time I'll see it. I should have brought Mom's dishes. Or packed them up in the barn. But it's too late now.

Jed rides Biscuit, a bandanna tied around his mouth and nose. He looks like a bandit from an old Western movie.

We don't turn toward Enderby, like we do on the way to school. I go the other way.

The sheep bleat and Candi runs circles around them, barking and yipping. Everyone stays together.

I'm not sure what I pictured when Dad said he had bought a farm. But it wasn't this. I feel like I'm living through the end of the world.

There's no one else on the road. I wonder if they all evacuated earlier today. Maybe they forgot to tell us. Before we arrived, there hadn't been anyone on our farm for years. Maybe no one knew we were here.

It's slow going. I look at the truck speedometer. We're traveling at about four miles an hour. It will take an hour to get to the turnoff. It might be fully dark by the time we get to the bridge.

I'm starting to have doubts about my plan.

About twenty endless minutes later, the wind blows up. The smoke clears a bit. I watch Jed and the sheep in the rearview mirror. When I roll my window down, I hear the sheep bleating. Biscuit nickers.

Finally we reach the turnoff. The sign reads *Trinity Road*. It makes me think of the Holy Trinity. I hear about that when I go to church with Granny. I can't remember what it means, though. Something about God.

I'm not sure I believe in God. But as I pull the truck over to the side of the road, I say a little prayer to Mom.

"If you're listening, Mom, and you can send any help, please do."

When I get out of the truck, the wind gusts again, blowing away more smoke.

Jed trots up on Biscuit. I pull out a jug of water and a couple of pans from the back of the truck. With the pans full, everyone has a drink. All the sheep, Biscuit, Itchy, even Candi. Jed and I drink too.

I check on the chickens. They're dozing. A couple of them coo when I lift the tarp. The rest ignore me. I drop the tarp back.

Turning, I do a head count. Candi has all the sheep cowering beside the truck. Jed has loosely tied Itchy and Biscuit to a tree.

Jed washes his hands with water from the big jug.

"Don't use too much," I say. "We might need it."

"The animals can drink from the river," Jed says. "We have water bottles for us."

He's right.

Before I turn us toward the bridge road, I take out my phone to call Dad. Just to tell him we're on our way.

But the phone screen says *No service*.

Chapter Six

A few minutes after we turn off the valley road and toward the river, I see flames for the first time. They're still far away, up on the hills. The wind whips around. And the flames seem to race toward us.

I drive faster. In the rearview mirror I see Jed press his heels into Biscuit's sides. She speeds up to a canter. This makes Itchy speed up. The sheep start to run behind. Candi barks at them, keeping them on the road.

The fire seems to follow us. It moves along the tree line like a living thing. Stalking us. Suddenly it's ahead of us. Devouring trees and scrub on the hillside.

Then a tongue of fire licks into a farmer's field. By the time we reach the field, it is nearly gone. There is only black stubble. Smoke billows into the sky. A farmhouse is on fire!

I hit the brakes. The animals flow around the truck. Jed pulls Biscuit up beside my window. I roll it down. The smoke makes me blink. Jed's eyes are red and streaming.

The air smells like everything is burning—trees, grass, metal cars, rubber tires.

Everything.

"What should we do?" Jed asks frantically.

"Wait here," I say, getting out of the truck. "I'll see if there's anyone in that house."

I pull my T-shirt over my mouth and run up the farmer's driveway.

"Hello?!" I yell. "Is anyone there?"

The fire creeps over the roof. Down the walls. I don't dare get closer. I grab a rock and throw it at the front door. *Bang!* What if people are trapped inside? Am I brave enough to try to rescue them? Or stupid enough?

"*Hello?!*"

No one answers. There are no cars or trucks in the driveway. They must have gotten out.

We probably should have evacuated hours ago. The farm Dad grew up on was in England.

I don't think they have wildfires in the same way there. Maybe he wasn't reading the signs. Maybe moving out here was a dumb idea.

So much for Mom's gift to us.

As I run back to the truck, something moves at the edge of the burning field. It runs toward me. A cat! It's an orange tabby with white patches.

When I open the door to the truck, it jumps right into the passenger seat.

Jed smirks. "What's one more?" he says.

The cat crawls under the passenger seat. It cowers there, glaring at me. I uncap a bottle of water and pour out a dribble. The cat creeps forward and laps at it.

Its whiskers are singed. Poor thing. It looks well fed. But it has no collar. I suppose when this is all over, we'll have to try to find its owner.

If we survive. The thought gives me goose bumps.

I start the truck. The sheep shuffle along together. Candi barks, urging them on. In the rearview, I can barely see Jed and Biscuit and Itchy through the haze.

Suddenly, ahead of us, a tree explodes into flames. It splits in two. One half crashes down on the road. I slam on the brakes.

"I'm going to turn around!" I yell out the window. "That farm had a private road we can try. It should lead to the river!"

I *hope* it leads to the river. We need to get to the bridge.

Jed and Candi get the sheep out of the way. I turn the truck around. The farmhouse is now fully ablaze. But the fire hasn't crossed the driveway into the next field. The road to the river is clear.

As the truck bumps down the track, I realize how random wildfires are. There are no predictable patterns. Some places are burning, some aren't.

I wonder if the fire will spare our farm.

Or us.

Chapter Seven

Our luck changes. A little. We reach the river. There *is* another track running back to the bridge. I turn onto it.

The valley road was bad. Bumpy and rutted. The farmer's driveway was worse. But the track is *terrible*. I clutch the steering wheel, trying to steer. The truck bounces and wobbles.

The crates bounce in the back. I'm worried I'll roll off the road. Or fall into the river. Since it's been so dry, the water is not deep, thank goodness.

Jed rides Biscuit along the river's edge. Itchy follows. Somehow Candi keeps the sheep from falling down the bank.

I can barely see through the smoke. At least the nearby fields aren't on fire. I can just see some flames ahead of us. They're a bit to the north.

Or are they?

The bridge is old. It's made of wood. It is rickety at the best of times. Dad says the government might replace it. When we get closer, the smoke clears. And I see the government won't have a choice.

The bridge is on fire.

I stare in disbelief. My great plan to save us has fallen apart. I stop the truck. I sit there, frozen in terror.

The cat crawls into my lap. Maybe it wants comfort. Maybe it wants to comfort me.

A second later Jed taps on my window. I roll it down.

"What now?" he asks. He sounds too calm.

One of the traits of Jed's disability is something called inappropriate affect. It means showing emotions that don't fit the situation. Jed sometimes laughs when I hurt myself, for example. He didn't cry when Mom died.

This time I'm grateful for his inappropriate affect. Because I'm about to panic. And if he was panicking too, it would be even worse. I close my eyes for a few seconds.

This is not an evacuation anymore. It's a desperate run for our lives.

I open my eyes and look at the river.

"Could we take the truck down there?" Jed asks. "Drive across?"

I'm doubtful. The water level is low. But there might be places where it's deep. And the truck is heavy. It could sink into the riverbed. Me, the cat and all the chickens would sink with it. What would Jed do then?

"We'll go on foot," I say. "There's barely a current. If the water gets deep, we can swim."

"What about the animals?" Jed asks.

"They'll come with us."

We have to work fast. I close the cat in the truck cab for a minute. I climb into the back and take the two chickens out of the small carrier. They're still sleepy. They let me move them into Candi's crate with the others without complaining.

Getting the strange cat into the carrier is harder. Jed tugs a bit of ham out of one of the sandwiches. That's enough to lure the cat inside.

I find rope and bungee cords in the truck. Jed helps me tie the crate and the dog carrier across Biscuit's saddle. Biscuit seems a bit confused. She's never had chicken riders before. But Jed pats her. She settles quickly.

The small carrier has a long strap. Jed slings it over his shoulder. The cat yowls. Candi barks. She's eager to get to safety.

I pack all our other supplies into my backpack. Food. My phone, which still reads *No service*. The truck's emergency kit. The flashlight. Our drinking water.

Jed was right. The animals can drink from the river. Hopefully, it won't make them sick. It would definitely make me and Jed sick.

We leave the truck and head away from the burning bridge. A minute later I find a part of riverbank that has a nice slope down to the water. Stepping carefully, I lead everyone down.

We must look like a traveling circus.

The river is only up to our knees. Jed leads Itchy and Biscuit. He is frowning. But he doesn't complain. Candi, Biscuit, Itchy and the sheep have no trouble at all stepping along the rocky riverbed. In fact, I think they enjoy the cool water.

Me, on the other hand? In seconds my feet are numb.

A sound roars up behind us. We pause, the river gently swirling around our legs.

Then all of us—humans, horse, donkey, dog, cat, chickens and sheep—watch as the truck catches fire and burns.

Chapter Eight

A few minutes later, the bridge is gone too. I can't believe how quickly it burned and collapsed. Charred chunks of wood float past us. All that's left are the concrete pylons, poking up from the river.

The sun is setting, and it's dark. The brightest light comes from the fire. It's all around us now, on both sides of the river. I click on the flashlight. It lights up the smoke in the air.

I lead us downstream. Even the animals are silent as we pass the remains of the bridge. Maybe they know they could have died there.

We slosh along the wide river. I grab a long tree branch from the bank and poke the riverbed in front of me. I need to be sure not to lead everyone into deep areas.

"Sheep wool is waterproof," Jed says after a few minutes. I expect him to go on. He sometimes likes to list everything he knows about a subject. LEGO. *Star Wars*. Different animals. But maybe he realizes now is not the time.

That sheep are waterproof is helpful information. Jed leaves it at that.

The river gurgles. The sheep huff and whimper. Once in a while Candi yips at one of them. But apart from that, we're quiet.

I think the chickens have gone back to sleep. Maybe rocking in their crates on Biscuit's back has calmed them. Maybe they're just stupid. I'm jealous. It must be nice not to know how close to death you are.

That makes me think of Mom, who knew for months that she was dying. I wonder if she felt like I do right now—both panicky and numb.

We walk for what seems like forever. I can't feel my feet. I poke the riverbed. Still shallow. We keep going. With my other hand I hold the flashlight. The light is weak compared to the licks of flame on either side of us. My throat burns from the smoke.

Where the river bends, I stop and shine the flashlight on Jed. He's soaked to his thighs. The animals mill around him. Biscuit and Itchy drink from the river.

I do a count again. Still eight sheep. Itchy, looking angry. He grunts as though this is all my fault. Biscuit noses Jed. Candi woofs. The cat peers at me from the carrier.

All around us is either darkness or smoke or flames. My eyes fill with tears.

"We can't do this, Jed," I say. I don't mean to. It just comes out.

"What choice do we have?" Jed asks.

"We could leave the animals," I say, trying not to sob. "Maybe just take Candi and Biscuit. We'll go faster."

As though it knows what I've said, the cat yowls from the carrier.

Jed looks serious. He knows this would mean some of the animals die. Maybe all of them. Drown in the river or burn in the fire.

"Let's keep going, Poppy," Jed says. "Just a little while longer." He whistles, and Candi nips at the sheep. They slosh forward. I start to lead them again, shining the flashlight. The river narrows ahead. What if it gets so narrow that the fire is close enough to burn us? What if it traps us?

I wish we had never left the city. Never moved to the farm. It was a dumb plan.

I wish Mom had never died. None of this would have happened! We'd be back in our comfortable apartment in Vancouver. Watching this all on TV.

I feel like screaming. Or lying down in the river and letting it wash me away.

We come around another bend. Suddenly, ahead of us, a tree rises up. It seems to be in the middle of the river. That makes no sense. I blink, shining my flashlight on it.

The river bend is wide. And there in the middle is an island. An island in the river! It's covered in sand and low, tangled bushes.

And no, I'm not seeing things. There's a tall, thin, scraggly tree poking up from it too. Smoke swirls around its branches.

"There!" I say.

We have to step carefully. The river is deeper here. At one point it is up to our necks.

Jed puts the cat carrier on his head.

Biscuit clambers up onto the island easily. Water drains out of the chicken crates. The chickens all wake up and shake themselves. I bet they were not expecting a bath!

Jed pulls Itchy's lead. Itchy swims to the island, complaining the whole way.

Back in the shallows, Candi barks, but the sheep are reluctant. Jed and I go back and yank them into the deep water. We half carry them, half shove them, one by one, up onto the island. Candi swims after us.

Finally everyone is on dry land. I do another head count.

Eight sheep. Twelve chickens. A cat. A horse. A donkey. A dog. Jed. Me.

We're safe. For now.

Chapter Nine

Jed pours water from one of the bottles into his mouth. "Where are we?" he asks between swallows.

Unbelievably, the flashlight still works. I shine it across the river. But I can't see anything. Just the dark riverbank. The dots of fire, now moving away from us. Smoke.

"No idea," I say. "Maybe halfway back to Enderby?"

Jed is shivering as he passes me the water bottle. The river water was icy. And now that night has fallen, the air is cold too.

The animals will be all right. They're used to the cold. Humans aren't as hardy.

I gulp the water. It feels good on my burning throat. For a few seconds I try to think.

"No one knows we're here," I say. I dig my phone out of my pocket. Water drips from its case. It's dead.

I knew I should have gotten the waterproof one.

"Dad will be frantic," I say. "If he goes looking for us, he could get caught in the fire."

There's still a faint glow in the sky from the setting sun. The sun sets in the west. I know the town is that way.

"I'll go for help," I say.

"No, Poppy. Not by yourself!" Jed says.

"Your job is to take care of the animals, remember?" I take Biscuit's lead. "If I ride, I can go faster."

"You're not a good rider," Jed says. He's not being mean. It's true. I'm nowhere near as good as him.

"Biscuit is a good horse," I say. I know he won't argue with that. "We'll be fine."

Jed helps me untie the chicken crates from Biscuit's saddle. We set them on the highest part of the little island. Jed helps me climb onto Biscuit's back.

"I just need to keep following the river," I say. I don't know if I'm reassuring Jed or myself. Jed leads Biscuit to the river's edge. I lean down and talk quietly to him.

"Jed, listen to me. If something happens and you need to leave the animals to survive, you have to do it."

"It won't—"

"Promise!" I say firmly. "You have to save yourself. Promise me."

Jed nods gravely. "I promise," he says. His jaw is set and determined.

Even though he's wet and shivering, he looks like a hero. Like someone from one of the rescue videos he loves. I know he'll be okay. I know he'll take care of the animals for as long as he can. But he won't risk his own life. I trust him.

"Be good, Biscuit," he says as I steer her carefully into the water. "Be careful!"

We splash away from the island. A minute later the river bends again, and the island is out of sight. Smoke billows over us. Fire glows in the distance.

Biscuit shies and neighs, but I hold her reins firm. She plods on, following the beam of my flashlight.

The river bends again and again. I start to feel like I'm going in circles. Have we been walking forever? Suddenly Biscuit stops. No amount of encouragement moves her. I slide out of the saddle. In water up to my thighs, I shine the light forward.

Through the smoke I now see the river ahead. It's gotten deeper and rougher. The water churns around sharp rocks. I was leading us into danger. Biscuit stopped us.

"Good horse," I say, giving her a pat. I tug her over to the south bank. It's still shallow enough to walk there. She follows as I pull her lead. We walk and walk and walk.

My feet are numb. My lungs burn. I don't know if my eyes are running or if I'm crying. I feel like I've fallen into a cursed world. Somewhere the river never ends. Where night never ends.

The flashlight goes out! I shake it. Nothing. We're in pure darkness.

Biscuit neighs, frightened.

Now I *am* crying. What am I going to do? I step forward an inch, feeling with my feet. Another inch. Forward.

Forward. My eyes droop. I'm dizzy. Like I've forgotten to breathe.

Ahead of me I see a light. It's faint. Golden.

Keep going, a voice says.

"Mom?" I say. My mouth is numb with cold. My lips are dry and chapped.

My brave girl, the voice says. *Keep going.*

"I miss you, Mom," I say with a sob.

I know. But you'll be all right. All of you.

The golden light is brighter now. I blink. The light turns white. It moves.

"Mom?" I say. She doesn't answer. "MOM!!"

I tug Biscuit toward the light. It separates into two lights. Headlights! Then there are red lights. Flashing. A fire truck!

"Help!" I yell. "I'm here! Help!"

A firefighter jumps out of the truck. Two others follow. They run toward me, down to the river. Just as they reach me, my knees give out. I fall face forward into the water.

Chapter Ten

One firefighter wraps me in a silver blanket. Another talks on the radio. A third one holds an oxygen mask over Biscuit's nose.

"We got through to your dad," the first one says a minute later. "He's on his way back to Enderby. Where's your brother?"

I describe the island. One of the firefighters thinks she knows where it is.

"Come in the truck with us," she says. "You can show us."

"The fire..." I say.

"The fire has already been through there," she says. "It won't come back."

I look around. The red lights flash on scorched fields.

Another firefighter ties Biscuit to a metal gate. He fills a bucket with water and lets her drink.

When they buckle me into the truck, I feel like I'm back in the real world. I escaped the cursed world somehow.

With Mom's help maybe.

We bounce along the riverbank in the fire truck. In a few minutes we're back at the island.

"That'll be it," the firefighter says. I don't know why she's smiling.

I lean forward and look out to the river. It's too dark to see the island. But there are six emergency beacons shining through the haze. They must have been in the emergency kit! Jed set them out. He knew what to do. Of course he did.

The firefighters turn the truck to shine the headlights across the river.

There is Jed, waving. The animals are close around him. Candi barks.

Relief washes over me. I swear I only close my eyes for a second.

The next thing I know someone is carrying me. I open my eyes.

"Dad!"

"You're awake," he says, grinning down at me. His face is smudged with soot.

"Is Jed okay?" I say.

"He's fine. A bit cold. They wanted to watch him at the hospital. But he'll be fine."

"He was so great, Dad," I say. "He remembered everything to bring. He was so calm. I wouldn't have made it without him."

Dad just smiles. He sets me down on a sofa. I look around.

"Is this the school?" I say. "The staff room? I'm not allowed in here."

Dad laughs. "Just this once," he says. "The gym is full. This is the only bed left."

I rub my head. "Full? Oh, like an emergency

refuge?" Lying on the soft sofa, I'm tempted to close my eyes again. But then I remember.

"The animals!" I say, sitting up.

"The vet picked them up with his horse trailer," Dad says. "They're all fine."

He looks at me, his face serious. "I told you to leave the animals," he says.

"I couldn't," I say. "Jed couldn't."

"It was very dangerous. Very brave. But dangerous."

"Mom called me brave," I say. I think I'm still half-asleep. "Is the house okay? The barn?"

"I don't know yet," Dad says. "I'll try to check tomorrow. Go back to sleep."

"Dad," I murmur, as he tucks a blanket around me. "I saw Mom. In some kind of dream."

Dad smiles. "Yeah?"

"She said we would be all right. All of us."

"She's right," Dad says. "We will."

DON'T MISS THESE OTHER ORCA ANCHORS BY GABRIELLE PRENDERGAST ABOUT SURVIVING NATURAL DISASTERS

THE WATER KEEPS RISING

A flash flood leaves foster brothers Zack and Peter, who both struggle with ADHD, stranded in their foster home after the rest of the neighborhood is evacuated. When their foster parents don't return, it's up to Zach to take charge to make sure they survive.

READ ON FOR AN EXCERPT FROM
AFTERSHOCK

WHAT WILL BE LEFT WHEN THE WORLD STOPS SHAKING?

After a massive earthquake hits, Amy finds herself alone with Mara, a half sister she hardly knows. Together they set out on a perilous journey from their suburb into the city to search for their parents.

Chapter One

Finally! It's the last day of school. I'm happy. Summer is going to be great. I made some new friends this year, and we're going to hang out. Go on hikes. Maybe go to the beach. I want to try to earn some money.

I'm in tenth grade. I mean, I'm nearly *done* tenth grade. I don't hate school, but I don't love it either. I go to a private school that's not very big. Only about 300 kids go here. Our class sizes are small, so that's good. There are a lot of rules. That's not so good. But they're not too hard to follow, I guess. And we don't wear uniforms. That's good too.

The school is far away from everything. That's bad. We can't go get junk food at lunch. We can't walk anywhere. Some days Dad drives me to school. Other days I have to take the school bus. That's also bad. But it's only on the days Dad works in the city. When he needs to leave really early. Like today. That's about half the time.

I go to a K-12 school. That means we have kids from kindergarten to twelfth grade. Sometimes that's annoying. The little kids can be brats. But they can be cute too.

messy. We don't talk about it much. I know Dad pays child support for her. And he sees her sometimes. But…yeah. It's messy.

Mara goes to the public high school in Abbotsford. She and her mom live near there. That's not very far from us. We live just over the river in Mission. About a five-minute drive from my school.

Dad calls it a "suburb." But really it's just a small town.

I'd like to get to know Mara better. I've only met her a few times. Once I sent her a message on Instagram, but she never replied. So that was that.

Families can be a lot sometimes.

"Amy!" Sofie calls out to me. "Did you find the other mitten?"

She and Peter walk toward the school. Peter has three Hula-Hoops around his neck. Somewhere, someone's dog starts barking.

"No!" I yell back. "But I found a pair of headphones!" Another dog barks, like it's mad at me for yelling.

I tug the headphones out of the weeds. Suddenly the ground starts to shake! Sofie and Peter look back at me. Their eyes are wide.

Earthquake!

I expect it to be just a gentle rumble and only last a few seconds. That's happened before. But the rumbling and shaking gets worse. And it doesn't stop. Soon it's like the ground is turning sideways.

Gabrielle Prendergast is the award-winning author of numerous books for children and teens. She won the BC Book Prize for her YA sci-fi novel *Zero Repeat Forever* and the Westchester Award for her YA novel *Audacious*. After years of working in social welfare and the music and film industries, Gabrielle began writing books when she became a mother, so she could work from home. She is the author of *Aftershock* and *Flash Flood* in the Orca Anchor series. Gabrielle lives in East Vancouver in a permanent state of "under construction."